Case of the Sinking Circus

by Aaron Rosenberg
illustrated by David Harrington

PSS!
PRICE STERN SLOAN
An Imprint of Penguin Group (USA) Inc.

For Adara and Arthur, my own wonderfully puzzling little circus—AR

For my wonderful sons, Chase and Nick—DH

PRICE STERN SLOAN
Published by the Penguin Group
Penguin Group (USA) Inc., 375 Hudson Street, New York, New York 10014, USA
Penguin Group (Canada), 90 Eglinton Avenue East, Suite 700,
Toronto, Ontario M4P 2Y3, Canada
(a division of Pearson Penguin Canada Inc.)
Penguin Books Ltd., 80 Strand, London WC2R 0RL, England
Penguin Group Ireland, 25 St. Stephen's Green, Dublin 2, Ireland
(a division of Penguin Books Ltd.)
Penguin Group (Australia), 250 Camberwell Road, Camberwell,
Victoria 3124, Australia
(a division of Pearson Australia Group Pty. Ltd.)
Penguin Books India Pvt. Ltd., 11 Community Centre,
Panchsheel Park, New Delhi—110 017, India
Penguin Group (NZ), 67 Apollo Drive, Rosedale, Auckland 0632, New Zealand
(a division of Pearson New Zealand Ltd.)
Penguin Books (South Africa) (Pty.) Ltd., 24 Sturdee Avenue,
Rosebank, Johannesburg 2196, South Africa

Penguin Books Ltd., Registered Offices:
80 Strand, London WC2R 0RL, England

ISBN 978-0-8431-9810-2 10 9 8 7 6 5 4 3 2 1

Chapter One

"That's awesome!" said Pete.

Penny Pizzarelli was trying out a new toy. It was a pocket periscope that let her look around corners.

"Come on, Penny!" her dad called. "These slices won't serve themselves!"

"Coming!" Penny shouted back, pocketing the periscope. She and her younger brother, Pete, were helping their parents during the lunch rush. Pizzarelli's Pizza Parlor was always busy at lunch, especially during the summer. Penny didn't mind, though. She loved the fact that they owned—and lived above—the town's pizza shop!

"Why don't you take a turn with this instead?" their mom told them both. She set a piece of paper down on the counter. "Your father gave it to me. It's Ms. Green and Mr. Fields's lunch order."

"Ms. Green and Mr. Fields?" Penny asked. "Wow, I guess they like each other now!"

"Well, they tied for first place in the vegetable show," her mom explained. "That may have helped."

Vera Green owned the local vegetable store. Mr. Fields taught science and loved to garden. They had both wanted to win the vegetable show. Ms. Green had been so determined, she'd actually been stealing books from the bookstore! Pete and Penny had helped the bookstore owner's son, Jake, catch her, but Ms. Green hadn't meant any harm. She'd actually been borrowing the books and leaving money each time. It had been another strange case full of mysteries—and pizza.

Pete had rushed back over. Now he was looking at the order. "A puzzle!" he announced. "Ms. Green and Mr. Fields are sharing a pizza. They each want four pepperoni. Ms. Green wants two fewer mushrooms than pepperoni. Mr. Fields wants two more broccoli than pepperoni."

Pete and Penny started to puzzle the order out.

Draw the correct number of toppings on each half of the pizza.

(Answer, page 62.)

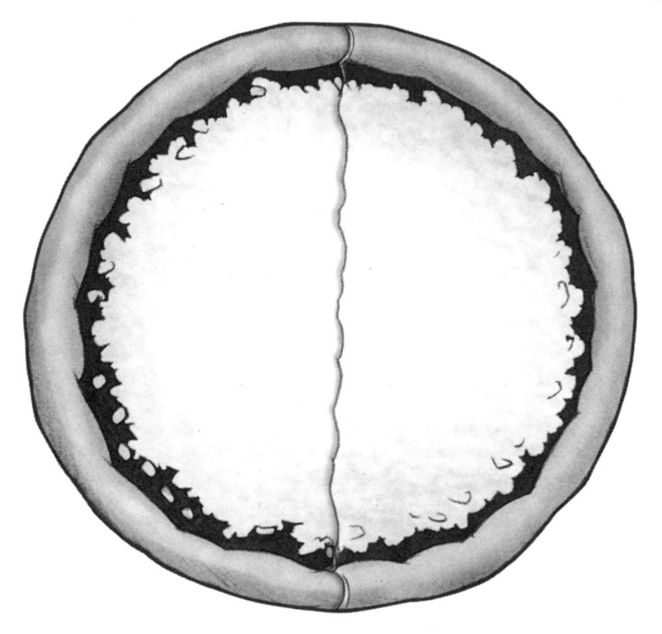

Ms. Green's half

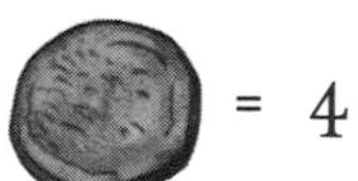 = 4

Mr. Fields's half

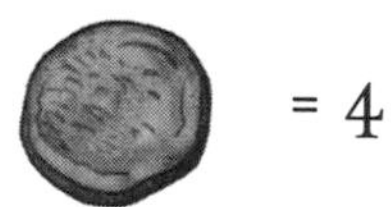 = 4

__________ - 2 = __________

__________ + 2 = __________

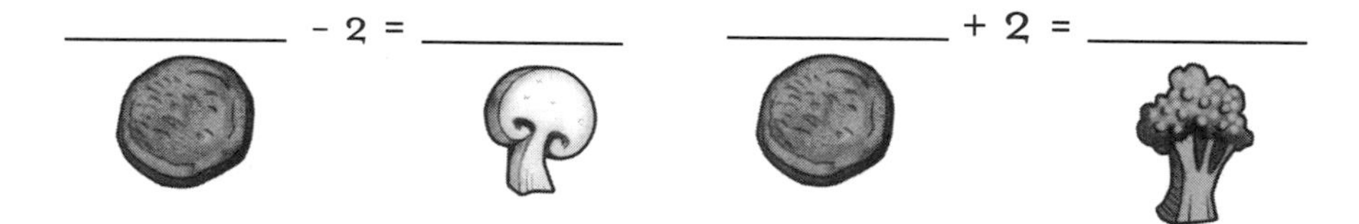

"Dad!" Pete shouted once he and Penny had figured it out. "We need half with four pepperoni and six pieces of broccoli and half with four pepperoni and two mushrooms!"

"You got it," Mr. Pizzarelli replied. He was back in the kitchen making the slices. Pete and Penny were taking orders. Their mom was handling the money. It was a real family business!

Just then the bell on the front door jingled. Penny glanced up as a tall man with a long, black beard entered. He was wearing a red suit and a top hat with red-and-blue stripes. The hat was so tall he had to duck to fit through the doorway! A boy and a girl came in after him. Penny didn't recognize them.

"Well, well!" the man stated loudly. He had a deep, booming voice. "What a lovely restaurant! And such impressive flatware!" He picked up a spoon from the Parmesan bowl and examined it.

Pete and Penny exchanged puzzled looks. What was so special about the spoon?

"My, my. I've never seen magnetic spoons before," the man continued. He held the spoon up in one hand. "Behold!" Then he squeezed his hands shut around the spoon, his fingers laced together. A second later, he spread his hands wide but with his fingers still meshed. The spoon stuck to them!

Everyone in the pizza parlor clapped. "It's magic!" Penny whispered to Pete.

"Thank you, thank you!" The man squeezed his hands together again, then separated them. He held up the spoon to show it was undamaged before setting it back on the table. "Ladies and gentlemen, my name is Eli Silkspinner, the ringmaster of the Spectacular Silk Circus. We will be performing in your delightful town tomorrow night and for four nights after that. Stop by the town square to purchase tickets starting this afternoon!"

Mrs. Pizzarelli approached the tall man. "You're quite the magician," she told him. "Now, what would you like to eat?"

"I'm afraid we cannot stay," Mr. Silkspinner answered. "We have to spread the word about our circus. Would it be all right if we left a few flyers?"

"Of course," Mrs. Pizzarelli replied. "We can even put one up in our window."

Penny went to grab the tape dispenser. Pete noticed that the boy and girl who came in with the magician were studying one of the frames on the wall. It held the article about how Pete and Penny had used their puzzle-solving skills to help their friend Jake solve the mystery of the accidents plaguing his dad's bookstore. The girl spotted Pete watching them.

"Thank you," Mr. Silkspinner said, handing a flyer to Penny. "Simon!"

The boy hurried over and handed Mrs. Pizzarelli a stack of brightly colored flyers to place by the register.

Penny was taping the flyer up in the window when the girl tapped her on the shoulder.

"Do you work here?" the girl asked Penny quietly. She was tall and had dark hair. Penny thought the girl looked like she was about eleven, just like her.

"We help out," Penny answered. "And right now we're out of school for the summer." She smiled. "I'm Penny."

The girl smiled back. "I'm Cindy. Simon and I help our dad and Uncle Eli run the family circus."

"Come along, Cindy," her uncle told her. "Everyone has to hear about the circus today since tomorrow is opening night. There are tickets to be sold, young lady!"

"I hope you'll come see the circus!" Cindy said to Penny as her uncle ushered her and her brother out of the pizza parlor.

"We will," Penny promised.

Pete had already turned to their mom. "Can we, Mom? Please?"

Mrs. Pizzarelli laughed. "Your father and I have to work," she said. "But if you can get someone else to go with you, then sure."

"I'll take them," Mr. Parcel offered. The mailman was just digging into an olive and pepperoni slice. "I wanted to go, anyway."

"Yay!" Pete and Penny shouted.

"That would be wonderful, thank you," Mrs. Pizzarelli told him.

As Penny turned to get back to work, she spotted a flash of bright yellow outside the front window. There was a man standing there, dressed in a green jacket and bright-yellow pants. He was peering in at her. Then he ran off. Penny frowned. *What was that all about?* she wondered.

Chapter Two

In the morning, Pete was the first one up. He raced downstairs and through the parlor. There had been some kind of noise outside. Maybe it was a package!

But when Pete opened the door, he saw a small monkey wearing a top hat. The monkey was holding an envelope in one paw and a bell in the other. That must have been the noise! The monkey bowed to Pete. Pete awkwardly bowed back. The monkey chattered. Then it handed him the envelope. The envelope said "Pete and Penny" across the front.

Pete started to ask the monkey about it, but then realized, *I'm trying to talk to a monkey!* The monkey scurried off down the street.

"What was that noise from?" Penny asked. She had come downstairs behind him.

Pete explained about the monkey. "He handed me this!" He waved the envelope.

"Let me see!" Penny was tall like their mother, so she was able to reach around Pete and grab the envelope from him. Inside was a single, folded sheet of paper.

"It's some kind of code," Pete said as they studied the page. He'd never seen anything like it. *This almost looks like ancient Egyptian hieroglyphs!* thought Pete.

"If a monkey really delivered this, then someone from the circus must have sent it," Penny pointed out. "We should look for clues at the circus."

Just then Benny walked past the front door. "Hey, Pete! Hey, Penny!" Benny ran the local coffee shop, Benny's Beans.

"Hi, Benny!" Pete answered. "What're you doing here?"

"Just taking a walk," Benny replied. "I like a little exercise to start my day."

Pete and Penny laughed. Benny was a bit round. Most of the time he sat in his shop and read books and drank coffee.

"We wanted to check out the circus grounds," Penny told him. "Just to see them setting up the tents and all. Would you go with us?"

Pete gave his sister a smile. "Nice one, Penny!" he whispered.

"Sure, why not?" Benny agreed. "I'm curious, too. It's very exciting to have a traveling circus in town!"

Penny ran and told her parents that she and Pete were going to the circus. "Don't get in the way of the circus performers," Mrs. Pizzarelli warned as they left.

Pete and Penny walked with Benny to the town square. The square was bustling with activity. There was one enormous, striped circus tent with a handful of smaller tents set up around it. People were rushing about. And they all wore crazy, brightly colored clothes.

Whoosh! One figure brushed past Penny and

caught her eye. It was a young man in a green jacket and yellow pants. *He's the one who was staring at me yesterday!* she thought. He looked surprised to see her there. Then he hurried into the larger tent.

"I want to take a look in there," Pete said, pointing. He walked over and lifted a flap to enter the main tent. Penny and Benny followed.

"This is unacceptable! Your swings must be higher, your flips sharper, and your catches smoother!" they heard a man yell. It was Eli Silkspinner, the tall, bearded magician who had come by Pizzarelli's the day before. He was shouting at four men and women dressed in red-and-blue leotards. "Everything must be perfect during tonight's performance! Remember what's at stake!"

"They know, Eli," a second man argued. He was shorter and heavier than Mr. Silkspinner. He had neat, dark hair and a maroon silk shirt over blue jeans. "Everyone's going to do their best. Right, gang?" The performers all nodded.

Eli didn't look happy. Then he spotted Pete, Penny, and Benny. "Ah, I'm afraid you're early," he told them. "You don't want to spoil the fun by seeing behind the magic, do you?" He shooed them toward the entranceway.

"Sorry about that," said Benny. "We didn't mean to upset you. It's just so interesting having a circus in town and all."

Penny noticed Cindy and her brother, Simon, standing near the heavyset man. Simon nodded at Pete and Penny. Then he walked past them and right out of the tent without a word!

But Penny's quick eyes had seen something fall from Simon's hand. She nudged Pete. He nodded. He'd seen it, too.

Pete knelt down and pretended to retie his shoelaces. His foot was right next to whatever Simon had dropped!

When he stood up, Pete had something hidden in his hand.

Outside, Penny grabbed Pete's arm. "What did Simon drop?" she asked quietly.

Pete showed her what he'd found. It was a piece of paper wrapped around a code key! The paper read "We forgot to send this with Claude. Can you help us?"

"Claude?" Penny wondered aloud.

Pete laughed. "Claude must be the monkey! He *did* look like a Claude!"

"Simon and Cindy must have sent Claude, too," he said as they left the circus.

"I guess we should head back," said Benny, walking toward the pizza parlor. "Thanks for joining me on my walk."

"Thanks for checking out the circus with us!"

said Pete and Penny. Then they headed home.

Back in Pete's room, they spread out the code key, note, and paper on a table.

"Cool! It's a code," Pete announced. "The symbols show which letters to use. Now let's puzzle out what this message says!"

Decode the message. (Use the secret code in the front of this book!)

(Answer, page 62.)

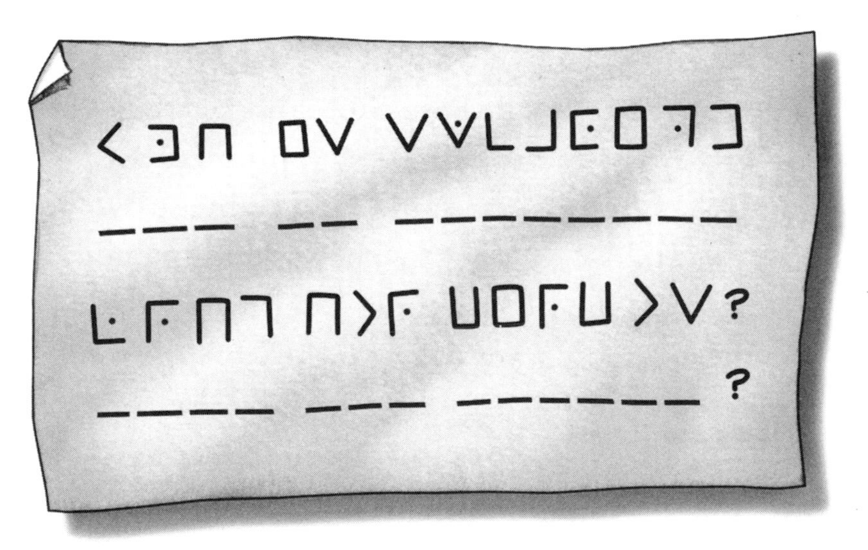

"Simon and Cindy *and the circus* need our help!" Penny exclaimed.

Chapter Three

"We need to learn more about the Spectacular Silk Circus," Pete said, chewing the last bite of his pizza slice. He and Penny had just finished their lunch—pizza, of course!

"We could ask Simon and Cindy about it," Penny suggested. But Pete shook his head.

"If they wanted to talk, they wouldn't have sent us a code key," he said. "They obviously don't want anyone to know they asked for help."

"Let's try the library then," Penny decided. She didn't really want to go to the library—she preferred running around outside or helping out at the pizza parlor. But the library might have information about the circus, and maybe the librarian could help them look.

Pete nodded and stood up. "Mom? Dad? Can we go to the library?" he asked.

Mr. Pizzarelli peered in from the kitchen.

"I know that look," he said with a laugh. "You've got a new mystery, haven't you? All right, go ahead," he told them. "But be back in time for dinner."

Pete and Penny waved and headed for the door. But just then, Mr. Parcel walked in with the mail.

"Hey, kids," he said. "Did you hear about the circus fire? It was intense!"

"A fire? Oh no! Is everyone okay?" Penny asked. She started to push past Mr. Parcel. Then she realized—*it's a joke!* "Oh, right, in tents." She laughed.

"Good one!" Pete laughed as well.

"Just trying to get you into the circus spirit," Mr. Parcel told them. "I'm looking forward to the show tonight!"

"So are we!" Pete agreed. Penny tugged on his arm. "We need to take care of something first, though. We'll see you tonight!"

"Sure—I'll pick you up here at six thirty! Bye!" called Mr. Parcel, but they were already out the door.

The library was near the town square—and the

circus. Pete held the door open for Penny, and they both walked inside. Penny went right over to speak with Mrs. Lender, the head librarian.

"The Spectacular Silk Circus?" Mrs. Lender asked. "We don't have any *books* on it, but you can look in our archives for newspaper articles that mention it." She pointed them toward the library computers.

Pete and Penny grabbed seats next to each other. Then they started looking. They both had notepads and pencils in hand.

"According to this article, the Spectacular Silk Circus hasn't been doing very well," Penny said softly, awhile later. She had found an article about circus troupes and other traveling shows. "It sounds like the problems began a little over a year ago."

"Hmm. And this one here says it was founded by Sebastian Vesilka in 1893," Pete added. He pointed to an article he'd just found. "Looks like Sebastian changed the family name to Silk when he started the circus. I guess so it'd be easier to pronounce."

"So do you think Eli is Sebastian's grandson or something?" Penny asked. "But he said his name is Silkspinner!"

"Apparently that's his stage name for his magic act," Pete said. "He and his brother, Martin, are Sebastian's great-great-grandsons. Martin must be Simon and Cindy's dad!" He read more of the article. "Eli and Martin's parents apparently didn't leave a will. Without a will, the brothers technically own the circus together.

Eli left the circus several years ago after

messing up a magic trick in front of a big crowd. It says here he was booed out of the ring! And that he only recently came back to the circus."

"Here's a list of all the Spectacular Silk Circus's acts!" Penny said, pointing to a file on her screen.

"If somebody's stealing from the circus, it's probably one of the performers who's been around awhile, right?" Pete said. "Well, now we'll have a complete set of suspects!"

Penny started scribbling down the names of the acts in the Spectacular Silk Circus. When she put her pencil down, Pete leaned over to study the list. Then he started laughing.

"What a mess!" he complained. "And why did you start with the lion tamer and then list the contortionist later?"

"I wasn't thinking about it," Penny replied. "I just wanted to get everything written down!"

"We need to put this list in alphabetical order," Pete told her. Then he grinned. "Leave it to me. I love lists."

Penny watched as Pete put the names of the acts in order.

Rewrite the list in alphabetical order.

(Answer, page 62.)

Lion tamer ______

Snake charmer ______

Contortionist ______

Trapeze artist ______

Magician ______

Sword swallower ______

Animal handler ______

Strong man ______

Clown ______

"Much better," Penny agreed when Pete was done. "Now we just need to find out more about each of these suspects."

"And about the circus's money problems," Pete reminded her. He glanced up at the library clock. "But first we'd better get home—and fast! It's almost time for us to meet Mr. Parcel!"

Chapter Four

"Wow!" Pete said as they entered the town square. Penny had to agree.

"It's beautiful!" Penny exclaimed. She admired the way the big tent glittered against the torches and lamps. Circus performers moved through the crowd in colorful costumes. Everyone was smiling and talking and laughing. It seemed like half the town was there!

Just then, something chattered near Penny's ear. She spun around. A monkey in a top hat was hanging from a tent pole beside her!

"Look!" Pete said. "It's Claude!" He nodded to Claude. The monkey raised his top hat.

"Hello," Penny told Claude. He grinned at her. Then he handed her an envelope. Their names were written on the front. The writing matched the writing on the envelope they had gotten that morning!

"Thanks," she said. Claude chattered again, then swung up onto the tent and ran across it. In seconds he was out of sight.

Mr. Parcel was just up ahead, checking out the cotton candy machine. Pete and Penny quickly opened the envelope. Inside were two tickets—and a folded piece of paper.

Pete snatched the paper and unfolded it. It was a maze!

Solve the maze.

(Answer, page 62.)

"They said someone was stealing from them," Penny remembered after they'd solved the maze. "It makes sense the problems would start with the ticket booth!"

"Now, where can we get tickets?" Mr. Parcel asked as he rejoined them.

Pete grinned. "This way!" He used the maze to find a small ticket booth near the big tent's front entrance.

"Ah, perfect!" Mr. Parcel exclaimed. He stepped up to the booth. "One, please."

"Wow, he's scary!" Penny whispered to her brother. The guy in the booth was big and muscular. He was completely bald except for his eyebrows and a thick mustache.

"I guess that's to keep people from trying to sneak in without paying," Pete whispered back.

The big man took Mr. Parcel's money and handed over a ticket. Then he did something to the dollar bills, but Pete and Penny couldn't see what. *Hmmm, that's strange*, thought Pete.

"Your turn, kids," Mr. Parcel told them, but Penny shook her head.

"We got ours already, thanks." She held up

their tickets to the big man at the booth.

He frowned at her, but waved her through.

Penny led the way into the big tent and pointed to the far side. "Can we sit over there?" she asked. "I think we'd have a great view of everything!"

Mr. Parcel smiled. "Absolutely!" He led them across to that side. They sat on the end of a row near the top. It really was a great view!

"But how does that help with the mystery?" Pete whispered after they sat down.

Penny laughed. "Easy!" She gestured to the way they had come. "I can see the ticket booth from here!"

"Nice!" Pete turned back toward the center ring. "You keep an eye on that. I'll watch for anything out here." He pointed off to one side. "Look, there's Simon and Cindy!" They were sitting with the heavyset man Pete and Penny had seen earlier. That had to be their dad, Martin Silk. He kept fidgeting and looking from side to side.

The circus began a few minutes later. Eli Silkspinner started things off with a few jokes and some magic tricks. He was funny, but only half of his magic tricks worked. Then there was Mr. Pride the lion tamer and the clowns and the acrobats and Steely Stefan the sword swallower and the trapeze artists. Next was the strong man, Muscles Malone—it was the guy who had been working the ticket booth! After him came more clowns and acrobats on elephants and then Madame Hiss the snake charmer. Finally, the clowns performed one last time, and then Mr. Silkspinner called everyone out to take a bow. It was a great show.

Penny was able to pay attention only half the time. The other half was spent watching the ticket booth. After the show started, she saw a man go over to the booth. It was the guy in the green jacket and yellow pants! He talked to Muscles Malone for a minute, and then the strong man handed him something. But Penny couldn't tell what it was.

On the way out, they walked past the ticket booth. Muscles Malone was there again with the man in the green jacket and yellow pants.

"This can't be right," the man was complaining. He was waving a thick envelope around. "The big tent was packed tonight! How could we have made so little money if we had so many people here?"

Muscles shrugged. "I put everything in there, like always," he answered. His voice was softer than Penny had expected. "Stamped it, too," he whispered.

"Are you sure it's all in here?" the man accused. "There should be a lot more!"

"It's all there, Ray," Muscles insisted. "Every penny!"

"Something's going on here, and I'm going to find out what," Ray warned. Then he glanced up—right at Penny! She gasped and looked away. When she turned back a few moments later, he was gone!

Chapter Five

The next morning Pete and Penny talked about the circus over breakfast with their parents.

"We saw Simon and Cindy," Pete told his parents. "They were sitting in the front row with their dad. He kept looking around. I think he was nervous about something."

"He must know that someone has been stealing from the circus," Penny pointed out. "He was probably just worrying about that. Or about having enough money in general."

"Maybe," Pete agreed slowly. "Or maybe *he's* been stealing the money and was worrying about his next move."

Mr. Pizzarelli shook his head. "Why would he steal from his own circus?"

Just then they heard a faint scratching at the front door.

"I'll go check," Pete said. He headed toward the door. Penny was right behind him.

Pete opened the door and gasped. It was Claude again! And he had another envelope.

"Good morning, Claude," Penny told the monkey over Pete's shoulder. Claude chattered back at her. Then he bowed and tipped his hat. Penny giggled.

Claude offered her the envelope. "Thank you," she said. The monkey bowed again. Then he scampered off.

"Is it another clue?" Pete asked after closing the door. He watched Penny open the envelope.

"Not exactly," she admitted a minute later. "But just as good!" She held up a pair of circus tickets for that night's performance.

"Cool," Pete agreed. "We need to find someone to go with us, though. And we'll have to get closer to the ticket booth this time."

"I'll bring my periscope, too," Penny suggested. "It might come in handy!"

"Good plan," said Pete.

That afternoon Rupert and Elliot Jest

stopped by for lunch. They were both tall and wore bright clothes, but Rupert was bald while Elliot had wild, red hair. The brothers owned the local toy and game store, Jest Joking.

"We're going to the circus tonight," Rupert told Pete and Penny. Elliot was busy eating but nodded enthusiastically.

"Really? We actually have tickets for tonight, too," Penny explained to them. "But we need an adult to go with . . ."

"It's too bad I don't know any adults," Elliot said, wiping his mouth. "But you can go with us if you'd like!"

"Great!" Pete grinned. *They really are more like big kids than adults,* he thought.

"Thanks, Elliot!" said Penny.

"Hey!" Rupert complained. But he wasn't complaining about Penny only thanking Elliot. He was scolding Elliot—for using his sleeve as a napkin!

"Sorry, it was handy," Elliot said. Pete and Penny both laughed.

That night the Jests stopped by to pick up

Pete and Penny. The four of them walked over to the circus a bit early. Pete and Penny had arranged it so they'd be some of the first people there. They simply had to get seats close to the entranceway, so they could keep an eye on the ticket booth throughout the show.

Muscles Malone was working the ticket booth again. He didn't say anything when he saw Pete and Penny walk in. He was too busy talking to Simon and Cindy's father, Martin.

"It's like trying to save a sinking ship," Martin was saying. "Nothing works! This circus is sinking!"

"You'll think of something," Muscles told him.

The Jests handed their tickets to the ticket collector. Pete and Penny did the same and entered the big tent, looking back over their shoulders at Muscles.

Penny looked around for Eli Silkspinner or Ray or even Simon and Cindy, but she didn't see any of them.

"Can we sit here?" Pete asked. The Jests nodded. Pete had found open seats just inside the front flap, right next to the entrance. From there they could see the ticket booth easily with Penny's pocket periscope.

"What should we do?" she asked her brother as they sat down with the Jests.

"We need to keep track of the ticket sales," Pete answered. "We know how much each ticket costs—five dollars. So we'll be able to figure out how much money the circus *should've* made from tonight's ticket sales."

"And when we hear how much Muscles *says* they made, we'll know if money is missing—and how much," Penny agreed. "Nice one, Pete!"

Pete kept a careful tally of the tickets by counting the number of people who paid at the ticket booth. Penny also watched the crowd in the tent in case anyone did anything suspicious.

Once the show started, Pete got to work. He set up a math problem on his notebook page. Pete loved math—in a way, math problems were a lot like puzzles!

"Each ticket costs five dollars," Pete said to himself. "So twenty tickets is one hundred dollars. That means every twenty people here means one hundred dollars for the circus. And I counted one hundred and sixty people tonight. That's eight sets of twenty!"

Then he closed his notebook. He couldn't do anymore until they found out how much Muscles said he had collected. In the meantime, Pete concentrated on watching the show. A big, brown bear wearing a small hat was on a red bicycle in the middle of the ring. The crowd was laughing.

About halfway through the show, Penny noticed a flash of yellow approaching the ticket booth. It was Ray! She nudged Pete to let him know she'd be right back. Then she slipped out of her seat. She went and hid behind the cotton candy machine so she could hear what was happening at the ticket booth.

"How did we do tonight?" Ray asked Muscles.

"Great!" the strong man replied. "We sold a hundred and sixty tickets tonight!" He patted the envelope. "And it's all here."

"Let me see." Ray snatched the envelope and started thumbing through it.

"Everything okay here?" another voice asked. It was Eli Silkspinner! He joined Ray and Muscles at the booth.

"Fine, fine," Muscles answered.

Eli dropped a coin behind him. Then he kicked it to the side. "Hey, you dropped something." He pointed at the coin. Muscles reached down to pick it up. That's when Penny saw Ray pocket a wad of cash from the envelope! He was the one stealing!

"There's only three hundred dollars in here," Ray accused. "Where's the rest?"

Muscles straightened up and stared at him and the bag. "That's not right," he insisted.

"There was more than that, I swear it!"

"Nice try," Ray replied. "But I know a thief when I see one. I'm going to speak with Martin about this right away." Then he stormed off with the envelope in his hand. Eli shook his head and walked off as well.

Penny rushed back to her seat and told Pete what she'd seen.

"So Ray's the thief!" he whispered back. He opened his notebook again. "Ray said there was three hundred dollars in the envelope?"

Use the key to solve the math problem.

(Answer, page 62.)

= $100

$

AMOUNT IN ENVELOPE − $300

AMOUNT OF MONEY STOLEN = $

"Wow, he took five hundred dollars!" Pete said. "And he probably steals the same amount every night. No wonder the circus is in trouble!"

Penny nodded. "Ray doesn't even seem to be a circus *performer*," she pointed out. "So why is he even here?"

"That was great!" Rupert said after the circus ended. "We should have a circus toy."

"Maybe we could make a toy high wire," Elliot suggested. "It'll be only a few inches off the ground!" The Jests started bouncing around ideas as they led Pete and Penny out.

As they were leaving, Pete and Penny heard two guys talking outside the main tent. "I saw those kids again tonight," one guy was saying. "We need to be more careful."

"Don't worry so much," the other guy replied. "Just stick with the plan. Nobody's going to be able to stop us."

Pete squinted to see who was talking in the shadows. It was Eli Silkspinner—and Ray!

The two of them are working together! But why? thought Pete.

Chapter Six

When Pete and Penny came downstairs on Sunday morning, Claude was sitting on the counter eating a banana. "He was by the front door when I got up," their father explained. "So I offered him breakfast."

Claude had brought them a new envelope. It held a single piece of paper written in the same code as last time.

Decode the message. (Use the secret code in the front of this book!)

(Answer, page 62.)

Penny sighed. "No tickets this time," she pointed out.

"Well, we *have* seen the show twice now," Pete reminded her. "And getting to the bottom of this mystery is more important than seeing the show again."

Penny looked up at the clock. "What should we do until three?"

Her brother frowned. "Why don't we look online for more about the circus or about its performers?" he suggested.

"Okay." Penny finished her milk and ran upstairs. She came back down a second later with her laptop and a notepad.

"Here's something," she said a few minutes later. "The headline says 'Talented Surfer Trades Board Shorts for Top Hat.' And it has a picture of Eli Silkspinner!"

Pete shook his head. "Simon and Cindy's uncle was a surfer? Wow."

Penny nodded. "It says he was good, but not quite good enough to win competitions. It also says that when his parents died, he quit surfing to help run the circus with his brother, Martin."

"When was that?" Pete asked.

Penny checked the date. "A little over a year ago."

"That other article had said the circus started having trouble around that same time," Pete reminded her. "I'll bet the money troubles and Eli's coming back to the circus are connected!"

"Well, sure," Penny agreed. "We know Ray's the one stealing the money. And we heard Ray talking with Eli about 'sticking to the plan,' so it sounds like they're working together!" She shook her head. "The question is, why are they stealing money? And who is Ray? We'll need more proof than these dates."

Pete shrugged. "Let's see how much Simon and Cindy can tell us," he said.

"I wish it was three o'clock already," said Penny. She just kept tapping her pen on her notebook and looking up at the clock.

After the lunch rush ended, Pete and Penny headed over to the circus. It didn't take long to find the elephant tent, either—they just followed the sounds!

Simon and Cindy were waiting for them. "Hi," Penny called out as they approached. Cindy smiled at her, but then nervously looked around. Simon just waved them over.

"Sorry, but we need to hurry," he explained. "Uncle Eli is off getting more peanuts and popcorn for the snack booth. He'll be back soon. Dad says if we don't make enough money while we're here in Redville, the circus will have to close immediately! That gives us only two days to uncover the crook. We have to work fast!" Simon led them away from the elephants and toward the performers' tents. "This is Uncle Eli's tent," Simon told Pete and Penny as they slipped inside the tall, yellow tent.

"We were poking around in here last night," Cindy said as they crossed the tent. There was hay on the ground and only a bed, a wardrobe, a standing mirror, and a few chests for furniture. "We think Uncle Eli is up to something, and we were hoping to figure out what that was."

"We think he's involved, too, but we don't have any proof yet. Did you find anything useful in here?" Penny asked.

Cindy shook her head. "Not exactly, but we did find this." Simon went to one of the costume chests and opened it. He dug through all the colorful costumes and feather boas in there. He pulled out a long, flat, wooden box.

"This box was our grandfather's," Simon said. "We can't figure out how to open it, though." He handed Pete the box.

Pete studied it. There were carvings all over one side. "This is a puzzle box," he said finally. "You have to figure out the right sequence of spots to push on. Then the box will open."

"Can you open it?" Cindy asked him.

"Maybe." Pete frowned. "There must be a code key somewhere."

Penny helped him examine the box. "What about this?" she asked. Penny pointed to several small symbols carved along the bottom of the box. "But none of these symbols match any other symbols," she complained.

Then Pete grinned. "You're right—they aren't the same," he agreed. "But we can connect them to the other symbols, like a leaf goes with a tree. That's it!"

Use the grid to figure out the code.

(Answer, page 62.)

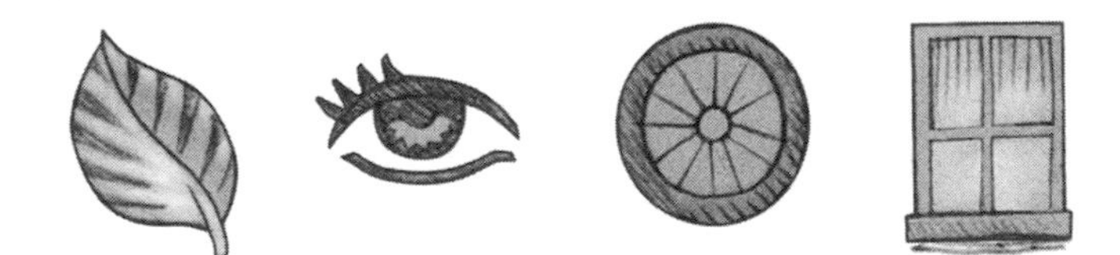

____ ____ ____ ____

Pete pressed each carving in turn. *Click!* The box's top popped open.

"You did it!" Cindy exclaimed.

Penny slid her fingers into the box and pulled out a heavy paper. It said "Last Will and Testament" across the top.

"It's our grandparents' will!" Simon gasped.

Just then they heard noises outside.

"Uncle Eli!" Cindy whispered. She took the box and closed it up. She tossed it back into the costume chest. "Quick, Pete and Penny, hide!"

Penny stuck the will in her back pocket. Then she and Pete hid behind the standing mirror. "Ouch!" she whispered as she bumped her knee. "There isn't much space back here!"

Pete shushed her. They could hear someone entering the tent.

"What are you two doing?" a voice demanded. It was Eli Silkspinner!

"We brought you some clean clothes," Cindy replied.

"Okay, well, run along then—I have work to do," Eli said.

"Oh, um, but can you come talk to Madame

Hiss?" Simon asked. "She's upset about, um, about that new performance schedule you posted."

Good thinking, Simon! thought Penny.

"Oh, fine!"

Pete and Penny heard Eli storm out of the tent with Simon and Cindy. They waited another minute before slipping back out from behind the mirror.

"Let's get out of here!" Pete urged. But Penny glanced back first. There was something big, heavy, and square in the corner behind the mirror. It was a safe!

"What's he hiding in this safe?" she wondered. Pete was pulling on her arm.

"We'll have to find out another time. We have to get out of here now!" urged Pete. He and Penny snuck out of the tent.

"We might need to ask Mom and Dad for help reading this will," Pete said as they hurried home. "It's full of legal mumbo jumbo, but I bet it'll help us solve the mystery."

Back home, Pete and Penny told their parents what had happened. Then they showed their parents the will. It revealed that Eli and Martin's parents had left the circus to Martin alone. The will said: "Martin, we know you love the circus as much as we do. We hope Eli will stay and help you run it, but we believe that our family's Spectacular Silk Circus is safest in your hands."

"Wait a minute! Does this mean that Martin owns the entire circus? And his brother, Eli, doesn't actually own any of it?" Pete wanted to know after they'd read it.

"It sounds that way," Mrs. Pizzarelli answered.

Penny nodded. "If that's true, then it makes sense for Eli to hide this will where no one can find it—in that old puzzle box. He doesn't want anyone to find out that he doesn't really own part of the circus. But we still don't know why he's stealing or why Ray is working with him. We don't even know why Ray is there at all!"

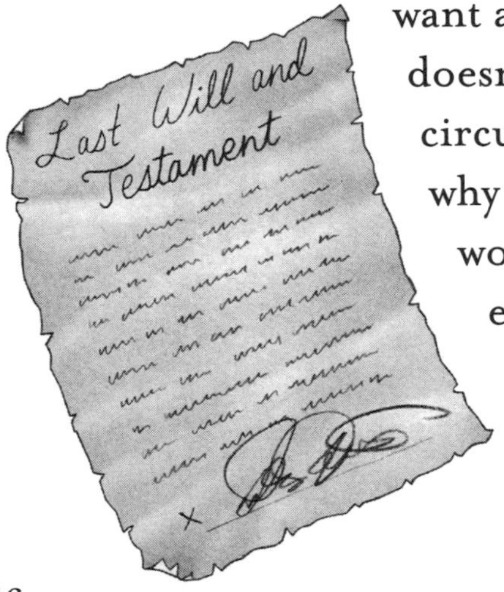

Last Will and Testament

Chapter Seven

"Okay," Penny said the next morning. "What's our next move?"

"It doesn't make any sense yet," Pete agreed. "We're still missing something."

"Why would he hide that safe behind the mirror if it didn't hold something important?" Penny said. "I'll bet whatever we're missing is in that safe in Eli's tent."

"Could be." Pete nodded. "We'll need to get into that safe. If we can figure out how to open it, we might find what we need to do to save the circus."

Just then their mom came in. She set breakfast down in front of them. "Could you help us prepare for the lunch rush before you head out today?" Mrs. Pizzarelli asked.

"Sure, Mom!" Pete agreed.

Penny sighed. "Okay, so we'll help out here

this morning. Then we go back to the circus tents between lunch and dinner."

Pete grinned. "Absolutely!"

"Thanks! You two have been a big help!" Mr. Pizzarelli told Pete and Penny that afternoon. The lunch crowd was gone, and they had closed the shop to clean up and prepare for dinner. Pete and Penny had handled all of the orders. They'd already swept and cleaned as well.

"Just trying to pull our weight, Dad," Penny told him. She glanced at Pete, who winked. "Is it okay if we head over to the town square? We can be back in time to help with dinner!"

Mr. Pizzarelli smiled. "Still working on that circus mystery, hm?" He didn't seem mad, though. "I used to love the circus when I was a kid," he admitted. "I would be over there watching the performers all day, too." He laughed. "If I didn't have things to do around here, I might sneak over there with you!"

Penny took that as permission to go. "Thanks, Dad!" She gave him a hug. Pete did, too. Then they headed for the door.

When they reached the circus, Penny led her brother behind the performers' tents. They snuck between the tents until they reached the tall, yellow one. They could hear voices through the side of the tent.

"Why won't you tell me?" a man was saying. Pete and Penny lay down on the ground. Penny lifted the tent's bottom edge and they peered inside. It was Ray! And he was arguing with Eli Silkspinner!

"You don't need to know," Eli replied. "I've got it under control."

"I just want to see how much we have," Ray insisted. "Can't you at least show me?"

"Here's the combination to the safe." Eli held out something small and white. "Help yourself." Then he snapped his fingers and the paper vanished! "Oh well, better luck next time," he said with a laugh.

"That's not fair!" Ray shouted at him. He stormed out of the tent. Eli left, too.

Penny quickly brought her head out from under the tent. She glanced over at Pete. "They're definitely working together!" he whispered.

"Yeah, definitely," Penny agreed. "And now we know the stolen money is in that safe!"

"How're we going to get in?" Pete asked.

Penny looked inside the tent again. Something white caught her eye. "Hang on!"

She wormed her way under the tent's edge. Pete was right behind her. Once inside, Penny ran over to the object. It was a slip of paper!

"Eli dropped this paper," she said as she

picked it up. "I think it's the combination!"

"He really is a bad magician!" said Pete, looking at the paper. "But it looks like the combination is written in code."

"Look! There's a tiny *e* written on the back of the page," said Penny.

"Good eye, Penny! It could be a letter substitution code, then," Pete guessed. "Those usually have some clue where to start replacing the letters. So, if *e* equals *a,* then . . ." He pulled out his notepad. "Let's puzzle it out!"

If e=a and f=b, what do the rest of the letters equal?
Fill in the key. Then decode the message.

(Answer, page 62.)

a=_ b=_ c=_ d=_ e=a f=b g=_ h=_

i=_ j=_ k=_ l=_ m=_ n=_ o=_ p=_ q=_

r=_ s=_ t=_ u=_ v=_ w=_ x=_ y=_ z=_

Eli Silk

_ _ _ _ _ _ _ _

When he had the answer, Pete typed the code into the safe. It opened!

The safe was filled with money! There was a folded piece of paper on top of the stack of bills. "What's this?" Penny pulled it out. "It looks like a deed for a house," she said. "Where's Wave Beach?"

"He's buying a beach house with the stolen money!" Pete practically shouted. "That's his plan! He pretended he was a half owner of the circus so he could steal money from it and then go back to surfing!"

"You're right!" Penny agreed. "But why is Ray involved?" She heard someone walking nearby. "We'd better get out of here."

"Yeah." Pete looked at the safe, the money, and the deed. "What about all this stuff?"

Penny glanced at her watch. "There's no time! People are coming!" she whispered. Pete frowned as they shut the safe and slipped out of the tent. "Tomorrow's the last night the circus is in town," he reminded Penny. "We'll have to talk to Cindy and Simon then. I just hope we aren't too late."

Chapter Eight

The next day Pete and Penny's parents surprised them with tickets to the circus.

"We'll be right back," Penny told their parents once they found their seats. "We need to speak to Simon and Cindy."

"Okay," their mother replied. "But hurry or you'll miss the show!"

Pete and Penny raced off, but they didn't see Simon and Cindy anywhere. So they ran straight to Eli's tent. They ducked inside and went over to the safe. Penny punched in the combination. *Good! The money's still here!* thought Penny as she looked inside.

"We can bring this money to Simon and Cindy," she told Pete. Penny grabbed a bag that was lying nearby. She started filling it with money. "Then their dad can deal with their uncle."

They heard rustling by the tent flap. "Quick, hide!" Pete warned. He ducked behind the mirror. So did Penny. But in their hurry they dropped the bag!

"Oh no!" Pete whispered. Penny shushed him. They waited for footsteps.

Then something chattered right above them. Penny glanced up. It was Claude!

"You scared us, silly—" she started to say. But then Penny heard something else. It was a man talking. And he was nearby!

She ducked back down just as the tent flap opened. *Maybe Claude had been trying to warn us?* she wondered.

"I'm still your father," she heard the man mutter, "and I'm still the one calling the shots. I hate it when he says that!" It was Ray! Eli must be Ray's father!

Pete tugged at her sleeve. "We need to go

before he sees us," he warned.

Penny nodded. She reached for the bag of money—but Claude got to it first! "Claude, give that back!" Penny whispered as the monkey grabbed the bag. Claude chattered at her and climbed up onto the mirror. Then he swung up to the top of the tent. A second later, he had slipped through the tent flap and was gone with the money!

"We need to get that back!" Penny wailed.

"Right now we need to get back to Mom and Dad," Pete corrected. "We'll have to find Claude later. At least Eli doesn't have the money!"

Penny sighed and let her brother lead her out of the tent. They snuck out under the tent's bottom edge and ran back around to where their parents were sitting to watch the show.

Pete and Penny tried to decide what to do next. *Who can we tell about Eli and Ray? Will anyone believe us without any proof?* thought Pete. *And how can we get that money back from Claude?*

The clowns were performing their last act when Pete spotted something. "Look!" he said. "It's Ray!" Sure enough, Ray was climbing a rope ladder toward the high wire. He was sweating—a lot—and kept looking up the ladder as he climbed higher and higher. Then Pete saw why.

"It's Claude!" The monkey was scurrying across the high wire. He was clutching the bag of money to his chest. Every few seconds, he reached into it and tossed bills to the crowd. The money fluttered down like confetti.

Penny caught one. "Look, this dollar bill has been stamped with the circus's name!" she told Pete and their parents.

"I guess that's what Muscles meant when he said he'd 'stamped' them all," Pete said. "That really is the money they stole!"

"And Ray is trying to get it back!" Penny couldn't help but laugh. Ray looked awfully funny trying to chase Claude on the high wire!

She saw Eli watching from the other side of the tent. He was laughing at his son's performance, too. Then he caught sight of the money. She saw him turn pale. He raced to the center of the ring.

"That money is mine!" Eli shouted up at the monkey. "Give it back right now!"

"It is not!" Penny yelled. She raced down to the floor. Pete was right behind her. "It belongs to the circus. You and your son stole it!"

Just then, Ray tumbled down to the net below. The monkey kept tossing bills into the air. The crowd was going wild with excitement.

"What's all this?" It was Captain Bell, the chief of police. He had been sitting in the front row. "Who stole what now?"

"Mr. Silkspinner and his son, Ray, have been stealing money from the circus," Penny explained. "They were going to buy a beach house and leave the circus for good."

"Mr. Silkspinner doesn't even own the circus," Pete added. "His brother, Martin Silk, does." He pulled the Last Will and Testament from his back pocket and handed it to Captain Bell. "Here's their parents' official will."

"Where did you get this?" Captain Bell asked.

"We found it—with Simon and Cindy's help," Penny answered. "They asked us to help them figure out who was stealing from the circus."

"They did?" Martin Silk asked. He had been sitting next to Captain Bell. Simon and Cindy were right next to him. "I had no idea!" He turned to Simon and Cindy. "You may have just saved our circus!"

"I think they have," Captain Bell agreed. He rose to his feet and stepped toward Eli Silkspinner. "I'll take it from here, though."

"Nice job, kids." Penny looked up. It was Ms. Scoop! The newspaper reporter was sitting a few rows behind the Silks. "I came here to write about the circus being in town, but it looks like I'll be writing about you again, too!"

"We're just glad we could help," Penny told her. Pete and Penny high-fived each other. Simon and Cindy smiled.

"Let's all go back to the pizza parlor," Mr. Pizzarelli suggested. "A good show always makes me hungry!"

"I wonder if we'll get another crossword puzzle," Pete said as they walked back home.

"Absolutely," Ms. Scoop replied as they entered the pizza parlor. She handed them a circus program. On the back she had drawn one of her crosswords. "Take a look!"

Use the clues to solve the puzzle.

(Answer, page 62.)

Across

1. Ms. ______ makes this puzzle.
3. What type of animal delivers messages to Pete and Penny?
4. Claude gives Pete and Penny two _______ to the circus.
6. Eli Silkspinner is Cindy and Simon's ________.
7. The _____ brothers take Pete and Penny to the circus.

Down

1. The Spectacular ________ Circus
2. Who is older: Pete or Penny?
3. Eli Silkspinner is not very good at _______ tricks.
4. Eli Silkspinner's circus ______ is tall and yellow.
5. What is hidden behind the mirror?

"We'll frame this puzzle once it's in the paper and hang it up next to the others," Mrs. Pizzarelli said proudly.

"Thanks, Mom!" Penny smiled. "That was pretty exciting!"

"Yeah!" Pete agreed. "We should have a circus come to town every week!"

"I don't know about every week," Martin told

them, "but we'll definitely be back!" Simon and Cindy nodded. Muscles and many of the other performers clapped and cheered.

"Well, in the meantime, how's this for exciting?" Mr. Pizzarelli asked. He slid a slice of pepperoni pizza in front of Pete.

"Awesome! You know I'm always excited about puzzles—and about pizza!" Pete exclaimed. He grabbed the slice and took a big bite. Then they all laughed.

Answer Page

Page 3
4 − 2 = 2
4 + 2 = 6
Page 15
WHO IS STEALING
FROM OUR CIRCUS ?
Page 21
Animal handler
Clown
Contortionist
Lion tamer
Magician
Snake charmer
Strong man
Sword swallower
Trapeze artist
Page 24
Page 36
= $100
$800
AMOUNT IN ENVELOPE − $300
AMOUNT OF MONEY STOLEN = $500
Page 38
THREE PM
ELEPHANT TENT!
Page 43
tree
face
bike
house
Page 51
Eli Silk
A H E O E H G
Page 59
SCOOP
PENNY
MONKEY
SILK
MAGIC
TICKETS
TENT
SAFE
UNCLE
JEST